The Talking Mango Tree

By A H Benjamin

Illustrated by Daniel J. OBrien

CaribbeanReads Publishing, Washington C, 20006
First Edition
All rights reserved.

ISBN: 978-1-953747-00-6 paperback
ISBN: 978-1-953747-01-3 hard cover
ISBN: 978-1-953747-08-2 eBook
Library of Congress Control Number: 2020919034

Peacock was strutting through the bush when he came to a large mango tree. It was laden with mangoes and well known for bearing the tastiest mangoes in the area.

"Yummy!" he cried. "A juicy mango!"

1

"Don't touch that!" ordered a voice.

"Who's up there?" asked Peacock, startled.

"I," came the reply. "The mango tree. If you want to eat my fruit you must sing!"

4

"Er, a-ll right," stuttered Peacock.

And he began to sing...

He sang high,
he sang low.

He sang softly,

he sang loudly.

He sang until his throat hurt.

"That's enough!" said the tree. "Now take a mango and leave!"

Peacock did as it was told and scuttled off.

The tree giggled.

Soon after, Snake came slithering along.

"Sssshh!" he hissed. "A tassssty mango!"

"Don't touch that!" ordered a voice.

"W-who sssssaid that?" asked Snake, surprised.

"I," came the reply.
"The mango tree.

If you want to eat my
fruit you must stand on
your head!"

10

"OK," agreed Snake, looking puzzled.

He tried to stand on his head, but it wasn't easy.

He swayed this way and that.

He wobbled round and round, but finally he managed to balance on his head.

11

"That'll do," said the tree. "Now take a mango and leave!"

Snake did as he was told, and he slid away.

The tree chuckled.

A moment later, Monkey bounded towards the tree.

"Oooh!" he said.
"A delicious mango!"

13

"Don't touch that!" ordered a voice.

"Who's there?" called Monkey, a little scared.

"I," came the reply. "The mango tree. If you want to eat my fruit you must do acrobatics!"

16

"If I have to," said Monkey.

He started doing acrobatics.

He flipflopped...

He somersaulted...

He cartwheeled...

until he was exhausted...

17

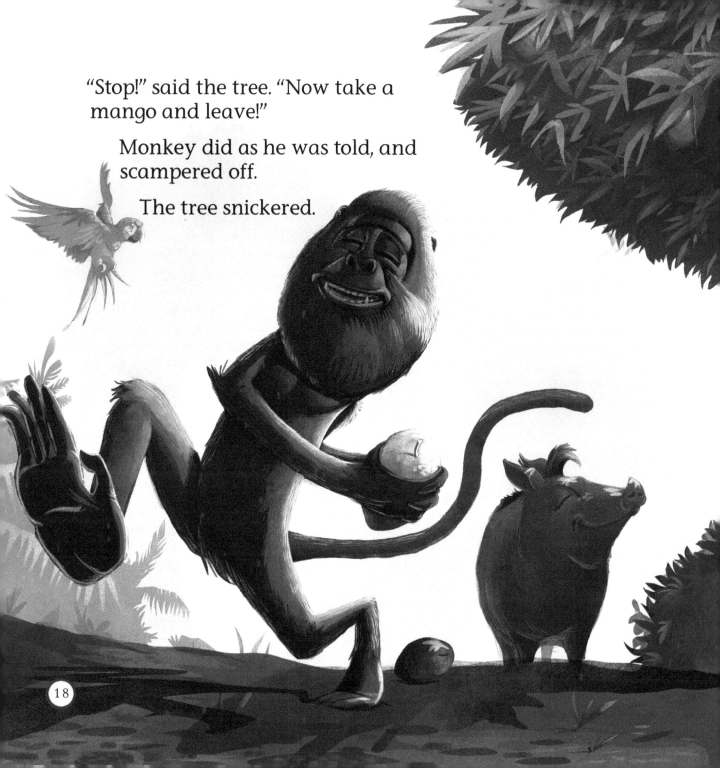

"Stop!" said the tree. "Now take a mango and leave!"

Monkey did as he was told, and scampered off.

The tree snickered.

Many other animals came to the mango tree for a tasty bite. But it would not allow them to touch its fruit unless they performed.

19

Parrot danced ballet.

Wild Pig skipped with a rope.

Dog juggled with sticks.

Lizard recited poetry.

Even Ant and his soldiers had to do a balancing act to earn a mango.

"This isn't fair," moaned Donkey who did not think he had any talents.

"And since when do trees talk, anyway?" said Bat.

All of the animals agreed.

23

Rumours that a mango tree had been talking soon reached Papa Bois, protector of animals and all wooded areas. He was not pleased.

"What?" he roared. "A talking mango tree? Not in my forest!"

And off he marched.

As Papa Bois strode to the spot where the tree was planted, more and more animals joined him. Each one felt excited about what was going to happen.

At last they reached the mango tree.

Papa Bois cleared his throat.

"What's this all about?" he demanded.

"I am the mango tree," came the reply. "You're not allowed to touch my fruit unless you do something for me."

"Oh really?" growled Papa Bois. "How about this then?"

And he pulled out his horn
and blew into it with a
mighty puff.

The mango tree shook and shuddered. All its leaves blew away. All its fruit fell to the ground. All that remained were its trunk, its branches and...

... a very scared Mongoose hanging on for her life to a small branch.

"Er, s-sorry," she said timidly. "I-it was only a joke... H-h-onestly!"

34

For a long time no one could say a word.

They just stared.

Then Papa Bois burst out laughing.

"Ho! Ho! Ho!" he chuckled. "This is the best joke ever played in this forest!"

The animals all agreed and joined in the laughter. The whole forest echoed with it.

"Come on!" Papa Bois invited everyone present. "Let's eat! There's plenty of mangoes for everyone! You too, Mongoose."

"Hurray!" the animals all shouted.

And they all feasted on the mangoes.

This time the tree did not say a word!

39

Lightning Source UK Ltd.
Milton Keynes UK
UKHW050849250321
380962UK00003B/16

9 781953 747006